Welcome to
Little Golden Book Land

By Cindy West
Illustrated by Mateu

A GOLDEN BOOK • NEW YORK

Western Publishing Company, Inc., Racine, Wisconsin 53404

There is a magical place called Little Golden Book Land, filled with wonderful things to see and do. Every day is a special day, just waiting to be discovered.

One bright and sunny morning in Little Golden Book Land, Poky Little Puppy was walking along slowly, sniffing the sweet red clover. Suddenly he tilted his head and listened. "I hear someone coming—someone with very soft paws!"

"Hi! It's me!" said Shy Little Kitten as she poked her head out of the grass.

Poky Little Puppy smiled at her. "Isn't it a fine day to be outdoors?"

"Yes, it is," said Shy Little Kitten. "But, you know, I'm so shy, I've never explored beyond town or my house in Homeway Hollow."

"I haven't either," said Poky Little Puppy. "My friends all come to visit me, but I'm too poky to climb up the mountain to see where they live. Wouldn't it be fun to visit Tawny Scrawny Lion and all our other friends?"

"Yes, it would," said Shy Little Kitten. "Why don't we go and see Tootle? He might be able to help us."

The two friends followed their noses down to Main Street. Tootle was just chugging into the railroad station with Katy Caboose right behind him.

"Oh, Tootle," said Poky Little Puppy. "Shy Little Kitten and I have never seen all of Little Golden Book Land. The mountains are too high for us to climb."

"Well, hop aboard!" said Tootle cheerfully. "I think I have some free time to take you there myself!"

"And I'll help!" chimed in Katy Caboose.

"Wait! I want to come, too!" called Scuffy the tugboat from the nearby harbor. "I hear there's a jungle with slushy swamps to swim around in!"

"Of course you can come, too!" said Tootle. "But how will we get you on board?" he wondered out loud.

"I know," said Katy Caboose, and she started to rattle off directions. "Poky, you grab Scuffy's towrope and attach it to the back of Tootle. In the meantime, I'll tow an extra cargo car over to the waterfront. Shy Little Kitten can open the back end and let some water in. Then, on the count of three, Tootle will pull Scuffy right in."

The friends all sprang into action. In no time at all, Scuffy was safe and secure in his own little car.

Then, with a happy toot and a whistle, Tootle
began chugging up the mountain. They passed lots
of things that Poky Little Puppy and Shy Little
Kitten had never seen before.

"The breeze tickles my ears," said Shy Little
Kitten, laughing.

Poky Little Puppy sniffed and twitched his
whiskers. "Someone is chasing the train!"

"It's me," said Tawny Scrawny Lion proudly. "I
love to race Tootle and Katy Caboose up the
mountain. Come and have lunch with me in the
Jolly Jungle."

The jungle was full of coconut trees and vines to swing from.

"Wow!" gasped Poky Little Puppy. "I could dig holes here for days."

"You're welcome back anytime," said Tawny Scrawny Lion. "But, first, won't you have a big bowl of my special carrot stew?"

"It's the best in the jungle," added a familiar voice as Saggy Baggy Elephant joined them. He lived right next door.

"Hey, Saggy! Do you want to play?" asked Scuffy.

"I sure do," said Saggy as he lifted his little
friend and plopped him down, right in the middle
of a mushy marsh.

"This is almost as fine as water," said Scuffy as
he sloshed around in the mud.

After a while Tootle gave out a loud whistle. "Come on, everybody! It's getting late. All aboard for the very top of the mountain!"

Tawny Scrawny Lion offered Poky Little Puppy a seat. As the train began to move, Katy Caboose shouted, "Tootle! Stop! Someone's missed the train!"

"Thank goodness you heard me!" gasped Saggy Baggy Elephant. "I was so busy playing, I forgot to get on the train."

Tootle puffed and chugged to the very top of the
mountain. The little group passed bubbling
brooks and deserted caves and hills that seemed
to roll on forever. Poky Little Puppy leaned way
over the side of the train to see better.

"Watch out!" warned Scuffy. But it was too late.
The wind whipped Poky Little Puppy right out of
the train! He was falling down the mountain!

"I've *got* you!" yelled Saggy Baggy Elephant.
"You're easier to catch than a peanut."
Poky Little Puppy held on tightly. "I'll never do
anything so foolish again!" he said.

Baby Brown Bear was waiting to greet them at the top of the mountain.

"I can see everything from here," said Poky Little Puppy.

"Little Golden Book Land is so big and so special." added Shy Little Kitten.

"It sure is," agreed Tootle. "And that's because we're all such good friends." He tooted a happy whistle that echoed throughout the land.